TWO LIMES

Calamities of a Young Manhattan Recluse

P.D. Famiano

Two Limes: Calamities of a Young Manhattan
Recluse by P.D. Famiano

Published by: Independently Published

Cover by: Vitelle

ISBN: 9781983357060

<u>Dedications</u>

This book is dedicated to the 5 women that helped me finish this project in one way, or another from proofreading, editing, publishing, design and reminding me to finish - Mom, Gina, Felicia, Candace and the one that reminded me constantly to release Two Limes, Lachelle Renness (Thanks for subtitles until 3 in the morning.) Thank you all and see you on the next one!

Table of Contents

Chapter 1

Americano

My name is Carmino Cartucci. I was born in New York. I know what some of you may be thinking already, and you're probably right. My dad is the very definition of a New York guinea. A short, hairy, hot-headed, crazy, passionate, domineering Siciliano -- to the core. He was born to Italian citizenship, named Valentino Cartucci in Mondello, Sicily, a sleepy beach town suburb of Palermo on western Sicily. The first male born in his family line has always been named Carmino. I think I'm about the 12th one now.

So hold on, before I go any further, full disclosure: This whole thing is some kind of experiment; I'm not an author or anything; and no, I don't journal or blog or any of that -- just hoping that if I tell my life story and somehow it's going to magically "Cure me of all the rage and chaos swirling round my head."

Speaking upon my life opens wounds, that apparently, haven't closed fully yet. I feel like I'm prematurely ripping off my scab, writing and rehashing out what I went through, but if my therapist says it will help me heal, then I guess I'll start picking at it.

Let's start from the beginning. I grew up in Hell's Kitchen. Namely, right about 54th and 10th, but on the 10th avenue side. The neighborhood looks a lot different today, but I always liked Hell's Kitchen, it's just not my home now. My father immigrated here from Sicily at the age of 21, not in search of better opportunities, and not in hopes of making a bunch of money and sending large portions to various family members, like the story always goes. Truth is, my father had a mouth on him and leaving Sicily was in the interest of survival -- move to America or become a headline. So after years of odd jobs in America, pumping gas, shoveling snow, menial construction labor, he became a bus driver for the MTA. This wasn't too bad considering his English was rather poor and his accent very strong, but he made a decent living off it, until a few strokes of bad luck got him fired -- the last event being when he hit my mother, then drove into the fire commissioner's vehicle immediately after. My mother wasn't too badly hurt, but nonetheless she was still hit by a bus and her foot was broken; my father had rolled right over the right ring and baby toe. He told me, "Your mother was the most beautiful woman I'd ever seen,and I forgot I was even driving."

The real story was my father had a terrible temper and was arguing with a passenger that wouldn't turn his music down on his boom-box. Those were the days of B-Boys and B-Girls filling the streets of the five boroughs; personally I always loved to watch them dance and hear "SHOW TIME!" when I would take trips with my mother to museums, the butcher, the baker, and an area off of 8ᵗʰ avenue where we'd buy our fish and vegetables.

Consequently, my father was fired from the MTA. He felt terrible about hurting my mother and went to visit her at the hospital where the two of them actually hit it off and fell in love. My mother refused to sue, which is unfortunate since the two of them later married and were quite poor, but she never thought making money from an accident was morally legitimate. "An easy dollar, is a dirty dollar," she would say. That was my mother. Some might call her naïve, but I only saw in her a human too good for this world.

My mother, Nadzia Ziolkowski, was a first-generation Polish-American. Her parents immigrated from Poznan, Poland and eventually settled in Greenpoint, which is basically "Little

Poland" in Brooklyn. There were latkes, borscht, stuffed cabbage and alcoholics...a lot of them. Somehow money was good, but then my mother's family became caught in the cyclical pattern of waking up face-down on the floor each morning and eventually you lose your business, your sanity, your gentleness, your peace of mind and in the end your family.

It's funny how we don't realize how much power resides in the most ordinary moments. It's these little bits of history, chance encounters, flitting fascination, brazen impulses that ultimately coalesce to mold the future -- they shaped my destiny, loomed over me all the days of my life.

The joke was my father had briefly worked as a gas station attendant at my Polish grandfather's place, but didn't have the courage, or English skills to speak to my mother. But my parents started dating, and eventually, ballroom dance classes and youthful idealism brought them together in a marriage that would be full of equal parts love and turbulence. Years of New York living made my father hard. However, the two were married and shortly thereafter I was born.

I recall many, late, coffee-fueled nights, as my parents struggled to devise ways to pay the rent. No one could ever accuse them of lacking in ambition, zeal or dedication. With the help of some colleagues, my father got into waste disposal and worked his way up, while my mother became a nurse. I spent countless nights alone in our apartment while my parents worked, studied and toiled tirelessly for an unforgiving city -- all to build some vision of a life they had for us. It's as though they shared this secret devout solidarity toward executing this mission, but in reality, the life they created was one of solitude, of alienation. Perhaps it was the violence my father had witnessed as a youth that made him so vigilant of me. Maybe it was the fact that I was their only child. My parents became completely over-protective. My mother's family was torn apart from disillusioned, delusional, derelict, drug-addicted, alcoholics, so maybe the fact that it was ultimately the three of us in a city of millions that made our isolation from the outside world so natural. As a small child I didn't realize I was isolated. When I would take trips to the market with my mother I was around people from all over the world. I listened to languages being spoken from several different cultures, sometimes within one Manhattan block. I was exposed to the theater, Carnegie Hall, Broadway and the slew of wondrous museums that NY had within its culturally vast dominion.

My mother would speak to me in the little bit of Polish she knew and my father spoke to me in strictly English, albeit his English wasn't that impressive, but he would shout at me, when I asked him to teach me Italian because he was of the opinion that "You're an American now, so you'll speak English and forget that nonsense of learning Italian." So there I was, an American now, son of a Sicilian immigrant that vowed to never return to the country of his birth, which he despised.

Chapter 2

A Lonely Boy from Hell's Kitchen

Although money was often just enough to get by in NY, my parents decided it was best for my mother to switch from working about 50 hours a week between two jobs in order to homeschool me. Within days of the conversation about my educational future at dinner, my mother cut down to one job, working 20 hours a week after my father returned from work. At the time I didn't really have an opinion on the matter. But if you think about it, it probably wasn't the greatest idea -- considering I didn't ever get to see my cousins and we rarely went out to the park. Other than the grocery shopping trips that I relished, I really didn't get to be around other children. My father never took me to Central Park, or any park for that matter. Most evenings when my father returned from work, he would sit by the window reading for hours, smoking cigarette after cigarette. When my mother left for work and he and I were alone, not a word passed between us. Don't get me wrong, my father was good to me, but he always seemed to be consumed in some type of greyish haze; his perpetual furrowed brows, grave demeanor and fatigued breathing painted a portrait of a man conflicted, troubled, and resigned. So I did my best to leave my father in peace, only speaking when spoken to, for I never quite knew when there would be that rare moment when I would find him in another semi-hallucinatory state, and eventually be forced to find his belt and "get one on the head." This pushed me deeper into my cave of solitude.

To my mother, I was her angel, her purpose, her everything. My mother poured an immense amount of passion into my schooling. I confess, there were times I questioned the value of an education where I didn't get to socialize, engage in discussion, and hear ideas from others, but I dutifully swept such thoughts under the rug whenever they arose. After all, I had absolute faith in the life that my parents worked so hard to create. I mean, surely, my parents' extreme anti-social seclusion was common and practical and certainly practiced by the majority of New Yorkers. In fact, everyone in any major city across the world most likely lived just as we did. Yes, other children in my neighborhood would play on the streets into the night, and the smack of a handball hitting a concrete wall would resonate through our open window, but those were the rebellious types. And I didn't mind being just the mere spectator from above.

I would always look forward to my cello teacher, Yura Adilov, stopping by the house twice a month to offer me lessons. Yura was an amazing musician. He'd studied at the Moscow Conservatory. While on a North American tour, he simply did not get back on the bus and stayed in NY. He spoke 4 English words at the time: Hello, please and thank you. Ironically, his first job was pumping gas at a station in Queens. It took Yura 11 years to get a visa. During that time, he was unable to go back to Odessa to visit his parents, even after they died.

I loved the time spent with Yura improving my musicianship. Yura would tell me about the great composers and he even gave me a small radio which would play cassettes. But naturally, my parents were always present, to ensure I didn't switch on the radio where the corrupted American youth gained access "to that horrible, ghetto, rap, criminal, shit music" as my father would shout. Instead, I reveled in the sounds of Bach, Beethoven, Chopin, Casals, Rostropovich and countless other classical icons. I'd close my eyes and let the sounds wash over me, envelop me, take me on fantastical journeys that I can only depict in colors: traveling through deep maroons, moody greens and vacillating shades of red and yellow, each brimming with sensations across a vast spectrum, full of radiance, then peace, then vibrancy, then solemnity.

We almost never went to the movies. But as a young, impressionable recluse, I came to believe that movies and television were where I could learn how to be tough, or a businessman, a lawyer, or a police officer, how to be a hero and how to not devolve into a villain. Nights when there wasn't homework to be done, books to be read, dishes to be washed, floors to be swept, instruments to practice -- compounded with bouts of insomnia...my mind wandered. I wondered how other children lived, how the millions of people that crossed through this island everyday lived, what they ate, how their apartments looked and if everyone of them took a shit into the Hudson. Would it make a poop island? I was a child, so of course, I often pictured millions of people shitting at the same time. I'm not sure if that was some perverse allegory, or if I just had a strange fecal fixation, but these were my most peaceful moments as a child, staring out that bedroom window, as my parents "room" which was actually the living room, orchestrated a symphony of comically violent snoring, against an endless backdrop of speeding cabs, sirens and cars honking as they sped up 10th ave. This was my nocturnal world as a kid. And I kind of liked it.

When you don't own a television, you have to get creative. The world beneath my bedroom window became my film screen; 10th ave was the stage and my favorite actors were the neighborhood regulars: drunks, pimps, pushers, tricks, prostitutes, gamblers, hustlers, thugs, junkies and every other questionable professional, namely the people my parents were trying to protect me from. But late at night, when my parents were asleep, that humid summer scent unique to Hell's Kitchen would suffuse the air, and pervade all the people walking through it with a lone kind of mysticism. And once I felt that, it was lights, camera, action -- my very own personal big screen, cinematic adventure sprawled out before me, with no beginning and no end.

Chapter 3

The Park

As my thirst for art, knowledge, history and music grew greater, so did the amount of projects and homework my mother had me complete. To me, I didn't mind all of the studying and trips to the library with my mother. The fact that my parents refused to get cable, or later in my teenage years internet access for our apartment, namely in fear that my mind would be corrupted, really didn't bother me that much. Time stood still. The fact that I wasn't exposed to such a vast part of the world, whether personally, or in an online realm, was immaterial to me, since one can't miss, or long for something that one has no knowledge of, or so I thought at the time.

P.D. Famiano

As I got older, Hell's Kitchen became cleaner, and my movies that played out in front of my window became a rarity. The sets were replaced with high-rise buildings full of people living a life of luxury. That became the word seen all over NY and apparently now the world. "Luxury living" was seen everywhere, in exchange for the artists and people of lesser incomes to be displaced, so that someone has a large glass window to stare out of, and a downstairs access to a place that sells $6 organic, fair-trade coffee. However, at the moment, that wasn't in my mind. Like any other young boy transitioning into puberty, I started noticing all the beautiful women NY had on this lovely island. Trips to the library, or walking to the market with my mother, I would be hypnotized by the legs of the countless women in office gear walking hurriedly on their lunch break.

How I longed to be in a public school, to be around other kids, other girls, but my father would hear nothing of it. "If you want to be like the losers on the street I see everyday, then pack your things now," my father would say anytime I would bring up the notion of joining a public school, or some type of club, or social activity, so I sank further into my studies and music. When I played my cello, no one could enter my world. There was no talking. There wasn't any stress, arguing, any discussion of the future, thoughts of the past, only notes, phrases, symphonies and most importantly, peace. Another form of peace came that Christmas when my parents got me a mountain bike, which was to only be ridden with my mother, never alone. It had to be walked about 15 minutes to Central Park and then ridden only there around the loop.

One hot summer day I heard a group of young women around my age laughing outside of my window. I saw a couple of young boys telling jokes and amusing the girls and I wanted to be a part of it, but instead, I just stared out the window, when suddenly it hit me, my mother was gone for an hour getting her hair done at a friends apartment and my father wouldn't be back from work for hours, so I decided to get on that piece of freedom with two wheels. I laced up my Chucks, threw on a helmet, knee pads, elbow pads, grabbed my bike and practically fell hustling down the two flights of stairs in our walk-up apartment. I hit the humid, hot Manhattan summer air and felt a jolt of excitement rush through my body. My right leg leaped over my seat onto to the pedal and in one swift movement I started to pedal up 10ᵗʰ ave. Since I had only been on a bike a few times leading up to this moment, I still had training wheels on my bike. I had no idea how ridiculous I must have looked, but I can't swim either, and always wear a life vest and at times arm floaties, so I was used to strange looks, but this must've been like an alien, even for NY. I'm a guileless 13 year old, horny young, sheltered boy with enough protective gear on to play hockey, and just to add insult to injury, I have training wheels on my bike. However, I didn't care. I flew up 10ᵗʰ, took a right on 57th, a left on 9th, right on 58th, whipped through by the subway and was flying through Columbus Circle into the SW corner entrance of Central Park. I was ecstatic at this point. I'd never felt so free and alive before. The feeling was like 10 symphonies going off in my head, mixed in with the thought of every gorgeous, long-legged woman I'd ever seen in Manhattan. I popped my first wheelie and nearly crashed, but I didn't care. I rode past the people selling kitsch gifts to the tourists and I was in the park. To me this seemed as exotic as exploring the Amazon. Completely lost in my world of excitement and forgetting how helpless I must've looked, let alone with custom training wheels, it was only a matter of time before some teenagers with little to do in the summertime, chose me for their victim of the day.

It was at this moment that four youth jumped in front of me, which I reacted in time by laying my bike down and scraping my ass, which was already delivering enough pain. Rather than their laughter to suffice their thirst and teen angst, they decided to let me know how stupid I looked, and just in case I wasn't sure, a few swift kicks, wedgies, punches and slamming of my head, luckily with my helmet still on, into the pavement. I think my first beating at the hands of someone other than my father lasted about a minute. Long enough for a broken nose and a couple of hairline fractures on my ribs. In typical New York apathetic to chaos fashion, no one came to my rescue, or even hollered at the boys to stop.

After laying there for several minutes I picked myself up and ironically was near the upper east side, not your typical neighborhood to get beat on the street, but then again, I didn't have much to compare it too. My bike was still in decent enough condition to ride home, which I went at a slow pace, since deep breathing really wasn't a possibility and only magnified the pain I was already in.

It had been about two hours since I had left home on a whim. My mother was sitting at the kitchen table with a frantic look on her face as I entered the apartment. She shrieked as she saw me walk in and then started hysterically crying and hitting me the way one would spank a little puppy that just peed on the floor. "Danny! What were you thinking? You had your mother worried sick!" she kept shouting as she cleaned my wounds and pulled a couple of frozen steaks from the freezer to place on my face.

We walked up the street to the hospital where there wasn't too much they could do for the hairline fractures on my ribs, but they managed to set my nose, give me a prescription for some pain medication and sent us on our way.

As we walked through the apartment door, one could feel the tension and anger that lived within those Hell's Kitchen walls. No sooner did my mother set the paperwork on the kitchen table, my father jumped out of his chair and started screaming at the both of us. After my mother explained what happened, my father looked at me with a furrowed brow and said, "You disappoint me, you disappoint me boy." I was sent to my room hungry, and never again did I have the urge to go on any more adventures, which only kept me more isolated and paranoid about my peers and the outside world in general, as well as confirming my father's suspicions that the U.S. and New York was full of heathens that did not contribute positively to society.

Chapter 4

The Lamest Teenager in Manhattan

The years passed mostly uneventful for me in my "high school" years in New York. While most kids my age were running wildly in the village, or at house parties on the Upper West, or East side, I was glued to my books and my cello. Considering most of my conversations, well actually all of them, with exception to a random conversation with my father, or a brief one with my cello instructor, I talked almost solely to my mother.

Having no idea how to converse with people my age, I felt to be in a self-imposed exile. I was so nervous being around other teenagers, but I knew eventually I would have to overcome my fear, just not now. Perhaps I would live with my parents my entire life. Perhaps my cello would take me around the world, but up until now I had yet to play in an ensemble, even though Yura strongly encouraged my parents at a minimum, to enroll me into a Saturday program at Juilliard for adolescents, since I was now approaching an age where enrolling in Juilliard itself was becoming a reality. I started to long for admiration from others. I wished to have friends my own age at Juilliard and music became an even greater focus for me. I would sometimes get lost in the hours of the night listening and studying sheet music of some of the great composers, only going to bed when I started to see the daylight enter our apartment windows.

Maybe it was my age, maybe I had spent far too many hours in our apartment, but I was feeling a building stress for independence, yet a fear of not being accepted in society, or of being robbed, or beaten again, which eventually calmed my longing to be like other kids, or come and go as I pleased. I decided to ask my parents if I could get a job somewhere a few hours a week. My logic being that I could help out with bills, learn to socialize and hopefully get a girlfriend. Within seconds, my father shot the idea down. His logic was it is a cold, dangerous world and after working so hard all of my life, why would I want to risk losing everything that I had dedicated my life to, just so I could make minimum wage by scooping ice cream cones, or selling some horrible clothes made by some little kid in China to a bunch of ungrateful teenagers. Besides, what did I know about selling, let alone clothes? I was an intellectual, not a fashionista, not to mention I tucked everything in my pants, but I dressed according to how my parents told me to dress. I'm paraphrasing here, but that was roughly the tone of our conversation. I walked back to my room sullen, yet convinced of my father's logic.

Eventually, I did convince my parents to let me get a part-time job. I worked the concessions at a local theater a few nights a week. I loved that job. Sometimes, I would tell my parents I had to be to work early, even though my mother would escort me to work, I would still arrive a few hours early and catch a matinee. Just being in the theater alone I felt a rush of excitement. I felt like I was an adult on my day off. I would make up elaborate stories in my head about leaving work early from the stock market and after having visited my mistress, I would treat myself to a movie, alone.

Needless to say I was a terrible conversationalist with my co-workers. I was always extremely nervous around the female employees that were close to my age. When I did build up enough confidence and told them that I was homeschooled, and what my life was like, all doubt had been removed that I was some sort of a freak, so any chance I thought I had at getting a date was completely out of the window. Also, when my co-workers started to realize that my mother, or father would pick me up from work, I definitely lost any credibility with my peers.

One day I lied about having to work, so when my mother dropped me off for my "shift" I waited in the bathroom of the movie theater for about 10 minutes, then ran around the corner. I cashed my check, which was around $100 and decided to explore. Being the great son that I was, I bought both of my parent's gifts. A nice hair brush for my mother, and a very fancy pound of prosciutto for my father. It wasn't until after I purchased these items and thought of the joy it would bring my parents, that it occurred to me, that they would wonder when I bought these gifts. Since my parents were always with me and walked to the bank when I cashed my check, I had to make up a story, but I never really lied to my parents. I never had any reason to lie to my parents. I didn't know what to do. Here I am a teenager in NY, where most other teenagers had already had sex, did drugs, had babies and traveled all over the 5 boroughs by themselves, and I'm freaking out over slices of a pig and a hair brush...but this was how my life worked. I decided to buy some gelato from a place my father liked and would take us to when he was in a good mood. This was splurging for me. I tried buying a cone for an attractive young woman and her friend, but they laughed at me as the sentences staggered out of my mouth. I was sure I was destined to be the only NY kid to be a virgin by the time they finish high school.

I sat down near Madison Square Garden and watched the masses of people moving frantically.

The majority of these people probably had major issues and concerns to worry about, and here I am, worrying about my obsessive parents and if I somehow have wronged them in yet another way, which will only, ultimately put me deeper in solitude. I took the risk and walked back to the movie theater where my mother was supposed to pick me up in a couple of hours. My manager at the theater seemed to take sympathy on me and let me into a 6pm show to kill some time. I don't even remember what I watched on the screen that day, I was so lost inside my head.

I left the theater and walked around the lobby counting the dots in each pattern of the old carpet in the main room. It was around this time my mother walked inside, with a face full of stress. She said she was doing fine and just not feeling well.

As we walked slowly home her face started to relax and she told me a story from her childhood. My mother would go to Coney Island with her brothers and sisters as often as possible in the summertime. Days would be spent eating ice cream, jumping turnstiles, since there were so many kids, they didn't always have subway fare and swimming in the Atlantic Ocean. My mother then started to cry and apologized for the life she had given me, and felt horrible for having me lead such an isolated life in the city that never sleeps. "Oh, my sweet boy. I was a terrible mother. I'm so sorry for how we've kept you so sheltered." I told her I had a great childhood and figured this was the right moment to tell her about not actually going to work today. I was after all 16 years old at this point, and basically never did anything bad, since it was almost impossible, if one rarely leaves the house.

My mother started to laugh. "Oh sweet one. You are such a good boy. If you knew all of the trouble your cousins get into in Brooklyn and here you feel bad about getting your neurotic parents gifts. What did I do to deserve such a special young man?"

"What did I do to deserve such a great mama?" I replied. My mother's face lightened up as we walked home.

She gave the prosciutto to my father and said she picked it up on special earlier in the day, to which he gave her a right squinted eye, as if to say "bullshit", but instead placed a few of those delectable slices on a piece of baguette and drank his espresso. I went to my room and practiced scales on my cello, before jumping into a Paganini Caprice 24 piece. Afterward I would stare out of my favorite window for what seemed like hours, before snapping out of my daze and going to bed. There is a lot to study tomorrow and "homework" to complete.

Chapter 5

Tipping Point

There seemed to be a growing tension in our Hell's Kitchen apartment. Even the stairway in our building seemed to be tense. As of late, my parents weren't speaking that much, or seemed all that affectionate as they previously had been over the years. The snide comments would become more frequent toward one another.

One time I made a comment about my father being too mean and unruly at times. My mother reached back and smacked my face. That was the first and only time she ever hit me. She began crying and apologized profusely. I told her not to worry. She told me, "One must never speak bad about one's parents, regardless of whether or not they seem fair and loving...family first Danny." My mother and father would often stress the importance of family. This was ironic to me since they both distanced themselves from their own families and I didn't have any siblings, but the phrase has stuck with me regardless.

When my parents would enter their screaming matches, I would sink further into my music. The sounds of my cello would take me to another world; a world free of stress, race, age, money and other isms that would keep us bound to this earth. Phrases and melody became my church. The classic composers became my prophets. The colors I would see with my eyes closed became more pronounced.

I'm not always sure why my parents would argue. We weren't rich, but we didn't have the burden of living month to month like so many New Yorkers. My parents did love each other, I just think their past had scarred them so badly, that even in the face of love they were skeptical and misled toward anger being a solution.

My mother would speak softly to me about my father being a bipolar, manic-schizophrenic. To me that was a lot of syllables and sometimes papa was mean and sometimes he was a sweetheart. That's not bipolar, that's being Siciliano in my experience.

"You're father had a terrible childhood." My mother would often tell me. "That's why he doesn't go back to Sicily and has no contact with his family."

"What was so bad about his childhood?" I'd often ask.

"Go play your cello, my sweet boy," was my mother's response to so many questions, but I couldn't disagree. I loved to play my cello. In fact, I was playing my cello one evening when my father stumbled through the door around 8:00 pm. My mother had prepared his favorite dish of fish and couscous. Contrary to popular belief, not all guineas like pasta, or eat it as often as society represents the fact. My father comes from western Sicily and there couscous is quite often more common to eat, than pasta. There were even times my father told me of huge couscous festivals with gorgeous women in costume, music playing as a soundtrack to plates being filled and emptied nearly as quick, all the while the camaraderie of friends boasting about each chef's couscous dish being the best at the festival.

I'll never forget this night as long as I live. This was and will always be, the worst night of my life. The scent of the alcohol emanating from my father's pores overpowered the delicious smells coming from my mother's kitchen. The food wasn't as hot as anticipated, nor as fresh, but since he didn't arrive around his usual time of 6:00 pm, of course the food wasn't quite as fresh. Nevertheless, this dish was better than any other dish, in any Italian restaurant in Manhattan, which unfortunately isn't saying too much, as most are not that good anymore, or run by Albanians, or Persians pretending to be Italian, all the while whipping up mediocre, imitation Italian food, but let that not detract from how amazing my mother's cooking was that evening.

Unfortunately, two of us did not eat that night. Where do I begin? How does one begin to explain the most tragic experience of one's own life. It took me a little over a year to even begin to speak out loud about that night and every night thereafter. I can't. Not right now. If I want to tell my story, or write it down, I'm just not ready. I'll try again in a week.

A week has passed and all of the sunshine couldn't erase my lonely, horrendous, ominous days, but I have mentally prepared myself to write about that night.

"Why the fuck is the food cold Nadzia?" shouted my father.

"Well, you're always home around 6 sweetie, I just assumed," retorted my mother.

"You just assumed. I am a man! You should and will always have hot food for me when I get home."

I wasn't sure how that would work, I thought to myself.

"Valentino! I'm not a machine that is here to wait on you beck and call!" said my mother in the loudest tone I'd ever heard her utter.

My father lunged at my mother as she turned and screamed to me, "Run Carmino!" "You're a monster!" she then shouted at my father.

"I'll fucking kill you bitch!"

I was frozen as my father pressed both of his hands around my mother's throat. She smacked him repeatedly, to which he sobered up and oddly enough began crying, not from the pain, but something of a wounded animal, as if years of self-hatred were released in that moment. He dropped to his knees. My mother was in astonishment, as was I. The two of us stood still. My father raised himself to his feet and profusely apologized to my mother. She pushed him off of her as he tried to kiss her and hurriedly walked out the door.

No sooner had the door closed, my father looked at me with eyes similar to that of a feral animal. "Don't ever be like me!" my father snarled and he too left the apartment within seconds.

I walked to my room trembling. I went to play my cello, when it occurred to me that I should go look for my mother. I threw on my coat and ran around my neighborhood for a little over an hour. I felt horrible as I walked up the flights of stairs to our apartment.

I saw a bottle of Grand Marnier in the living room. This was my father's favorite drink of choice. It occurred to me that I'd never tasted alcohol at this point in my life, as I removed the cork from the bottle and took a large swig. The burn in my throat that ran south was intense, but I took another big swig and then another. I went to my room and within 10 minutes my body felt on fire, so I decided to take another large swig and go looking for my mother again.

At this point the alcohol had taken over my body as I drifted down 10th avenue and cut over to 9th and 50th st. I zig-zagged the streets, occasionally calling out my mothers name. I was gone for a little over two hours when I decided to return home and go to sleep.

Sleep never came that night and to this day I still have trouble sleeping through the night. As I approached our apartment building I saw several police vehicles outside of our building and two ambulances. I started to move at a brisk pace and ran up the stairs falling into our doorway, as a police officer grabbed me, but I had already seen too much. Our living room was in shambles. There was blood all over our couch. Broken items were strewn about the living room floor. I started crying hysterically demanding answers, when two officers approached me and walked me downstairs. The officers sat me in their squad car and a few minutes later one brought me a hot cocoa.

They began asking me a series of questions and questioned me as to why there was alcohol on my breath. I told them everything about the night's events. It was around this time I saw my father run into our building and I could hear his screams from outside of the building. My father was escorted downstairs and sat into another police vehicle.

About 15 minutes later I was told we would all be going to the police station, where I would eventually be able to see my father. A few hours after arriving at the station, my father and I left the police precinct as the hour was approaching 3:00 a.m. Unsure of where to go, as we weren't allowed to return home yet, my father and I stopped in a diner and silently drank our coffee. The only sound to be heard in the nearly two hours we sat there was my father's perpetual whimper. We locked eyes only once and I wondered if mine were the same color of deep scarlet as his.

Finally, my father spoke. "I will never get a father of the year award, but you know I love you deeply Carmino." This was the first time my father ever said he loved me aloud. "I need you to stay strong, for your mother."

My father began to tell me what happened. It was suspected that after my mother left, she stopped in a bar to get a drink, whereas she was presumed to be followed home and as the perpetrator forced his way into the apartment my mother fought tenaciously, but the man proved to be too strong for her. The assailant raped my mother and severely beat her, then strangled her to death. Neighbors reported sounds of violence and screaming to the police and by the time the police arrived, the murderer was gone. The apartment door was left open and the body of my mother lay face down in a pool of blood on the living room carpet.

The night was surreal at this point and upon hearing this story I could feel bile moving north in my esophagus, so I ran to the bathroom of the diner and vomited heavily. Everything was spinning. I felt dizzy. I couldn't stand. My world had crashed before me. My mother was my best friend, and to know that an angel on Earth died such a disgusting, violent death, in our own home of all places, was too much for my young mind to fathom.

My father walked into the bathroom and held his hand out to me. I jumped into his chest and started sobbing hysterically. It might have been minutes, or seconds we stood like that in that diner on 9th avenue. It wasn't until the door opened, that we separated from our embrace. I didn't want to let go of my father. This was the longest and most definitive hug my father ever gave me. However, why did his love only begin to show in the face of such an evil tragedy?

We walked out of the diner and went to a hotel where a friend of my father was the manager. Arturo was from Palermo. He was a large, dark, extremely hairy and gentle man. Arturo was already outside of the main entrance waiting for us as we approached the hotel. He wrapped his arm around me as we greeted and a tear drop of his landed on my forehead. We walked silently as we proceeded to our room. Once inside, I sat quietly on one of the beds. I understood a fraction of the dialect Arturo and my father spoke. My thoughts were racing and I felt a fit of nauseousness coming on again. I ran to the bathroom and dry heaved until sweat rolled into my eyes. I splashed water on my face and laid down on the striped comforter in my clothes as my father and Arturo continued to talk. Arturo had pulled out a bottle of homemade grappa and the two drank quietly. I pretended to be asleep as I put my back to them and left my eyes open staring at the wall. I listened to them talk for hours and eventually Arturo left and my father just sat in a chair staring out of the window.

We stayed in that hotel for a week and reluctantly moved back into our apartment. There were no solid leads in finding the killer and each day that passed I believed we were further from finding the coward.

My father and I looked at each other as we walked into our apartment. Someone, maybe Arturo, had hired a professional cleaning service and the apartment was extremely clean. The majority of the furniture that had been in the living room had now been replaced with simple, modern furniture. There were purple Orchids on a glass coffee table. Purple Orchids were my mother's favorite flower. We both burst into tears and my father grabbed me and pulled me into his chest, sobbing words that I could not understand.

I finally received the affection from my father that I had longed for my whole life, it was just so unfortunate how I earned this new found expression of his love.

Chapter 6

Never The Same Again

Everything I saw, touched, tasted, and heard…was emptiness. I would often catch myself staring into the abyss, the floor, at a wall, anything, but often staring for what could have been several minutes. I noticed walking down hallways that I would hear and feel voices that would tell me to join my mother. The evil spirits were all around me. I had no ambition to study, or play my cello. Since my mother was my teacher, there was no school. I felt numb to everything.

My father and I barely spoke. We hardly saw each other over the next month or so and when we did, our eyes could barely make contact. I would cook for my father and I, but he barely ate. Instead, he was drinking a lot of Grappa and chain smoking when he would get home from work.

His gait was that of someone on large amounts of sedatives. The look on his face was a mixture of anguish, anger and detachment. His eyes didn't even look human, almost animal-like and distant, so distant, as if he were no longer on Earth. He never yelled anymore. I actually missed my father yelling at me. He spoke just barely above a whisper.

"Papa! Dinner is ready." I made gnocchi with sausage and mushroom sauce, which was one of his favorite fall dishes.

"You eat sonny-boy. I'm not hungry."

"Papa. You have to eat. You haven't had dinner in four days and you seem to be losing a lot of weight."

"Well, I'm a short, fat Sicilian, so that's good. Thank you. Now go eat Carmen."

"Ok Papa. Dad?"

"Yes son."

"They'll catch that animal right?"

"Yes son."

"We're gonna be ok, right papa?"

"Yes son."

There still weren't any solid leads on catching that evil monster that murdered my mother. With every day that passed, my hope that the police would find the killer was dissipating. My father's eyes seemed to be perpetually glazed over. I would take sips of his Grand Marnier more frequently and play my cello with my buzzed to drunk passion.

My father and I were lost and a mess. We lived in the apartment where my mother was murdered. My eyes would often drift to the living room floor where the body of my mother laid in a pool of her own precious blood. It was clear this couldn't go on forever, so I mentioned my feelings to my father and he said he would sell the apartment as soon as it was possible. He'd mentioned he had a friend that lived in Woodstock, and was thinking of getting a little house up there. I told him that sounds peaceful, but I wanted to go to Juilliard, and music was the only thing that made life tolerable.

Every day was full of emptiness, anger, hate, hallucinations and loathing. I felt I'd failed my family. The only two people in my life that were important to me were crumbling. I was lost. Some days it was hard to even get out of bed. Had it not been for my bladder, I probably would have stayed all day in bed.

I would have people on the street, or in shops tell me, "Smile, life isn't that bad!" Life isn't that bad. It's true. However, mine was. My best friend, my mother had been murdered and there were no strong leads to solve the case. I couldn't see light anywhere. My father was kinder nowadays, but he was also understandably aloof, and simply not mentally present.

This emptiness continued for a month more, or so. The house was littered and a slight a slight stench of body odor was emitting from our apartment. I felt hollow. My eyelids felt weighted with pressure, the kind of pressure that only a survivor of a violent crime can be familiar with. There is mourning for natural death of old age and there is mourning from senseless death, the latter which carries guilt for two lifetimes that ages a person beyond their natural years. That emptiness and loneliness will put you in dangerous, sad, pathetic, disgusting and lonely situations where a complete lack of self love, self-regard and just plain self is absent. That mind state that adheres to the demonic voice that says "drink this, sniff this, smoke that, do that, do that, do that"…and I would.

It was only when I woke up to being gently kicked by NYPD on the Staten Island Ferry around 5 in the morning that I knew I had to get it together. I was drunk beyond belief, and not quite sure how I ended up there to begin with. My father had stopped disciplining me. We were completely lost souls. I hadn't been doing any homework, studying, or even having the slightest interest in school. I couldn't see a point. I figured I would play my cello on the street, live meager, go to the library and that would roughly be my life, for the rest of eternity.

I felt cold. I felt empty. I was full of anger and hate. Everyone in the neighborhood looked like my enemy. I would walk the two blocks to the local market and do the shopping and cooking for my father. I still worked at the movie theater to make some extra money. Other than that, all I did was sit in my room and read, listen to the radio, or play cello. This went on for at least 6 weeks, maybe two months.

I knew I had to finish high school, so I took my GED. Luckily, my cello teacher, who was like family at this point, saw the chaos in our lives and helped me get an audition at Juilliard. The audition was in roughly three months. Yura stopped charging me for lessons.

He said, "Carmen, don't be silly. I'm your friend and teacher. I'm a horrible cook, so pay in dinner."

Between the knowledge of my parents that had been handed down to me in the kitchen I could definitely hold my own. Twice a week Yura would come over for cello lessons and afterward we would eat and talk for an hour, or two. Sometimes, even my father would eat with us and talk a bit. They would have great conversations about Italian architecture. This was a time that I think my father truly enjoyed and made him feel like an intellectual. My father would even cross his legs like a Parisian smoking a cigarette. I'd never been to Paris, but sometimes in the cafes here in NY, I would see people sitting and smoking and pretend I was in Europe.

However, when the silence arrives, the trips down hallways become a breeding ground for the most negative, self-defeating thoughts. At times I could see transparent spirits flying around me and if I listened closely, I could hear their high-pitch voices seething with temptation to jump from the nearest bridge, balcony, or rooftop.

The first few weeks after my mother passed I'd see transparent images of her for a few fleeting seconds. Paranoid, I was losing my mind, I kept these visions to myself, so as not to worry my father.

I believe my father was starting to slowly crumble from the inside as well. I returned from work around 10:00 pm to find my father sobbing in a fetal position, muttering words that were incomprehensible. I turned on a small lamp and put my right hand on my father's shoulder. He was trembling and his eyes didn't look human. Both of his hands were shaking.

"Papa! Papa! What's wrong?"

He looked at me and snarled, "I didn't want to kill him, but I had to."

I was in shock and confused. The only thing I could think of was he meant my mother's killer.

"Who Papa?"

"That little boy. He was so young. So young."

"Which little boy Papa?"

"He was sent for me. He, he, he ambushed me," my father stuttered the words out.

"Papa! What are you talking about?"

"Before I came to the U.S. I was working some construction jobs and there was an argument I had with some well to do people. As I was leaving work one night, a young man ambushed me. It was him, or me, so I strangled him until he stopped moving. I saw his eyes bulging and I swear I watched the soul fly from his lifeless body."

I didn't know what to say. What do you do when your father tells you he killed someone?

After a few moments of silence and watching my father tremble. I asked, "So, what happened next papa?"

"This man, this, young man, turned out to be family from some very dangerous people in Palermo. I knew I had to leave, but I feared for revenge on my family. Omerta is a very real thing Carmen."

I knew a little what this meant. Basically, no police are ever called in any discrepancy between two people. Even your worst enemy, you will not call the police upon. You will handle it yourself, however the situation deems fit.

"Carmen, I left Sicilia within a week. My sister Lucia was killed the following week. It was very brutal. This is a big reason why I struggle so much as a parent. The older you got, I just kept seeing this young man's face in you. Now this. Now everything. I can't live in this place anymore. This is not my home. I can't wait to leave this Earth Carmen. You are a man now. You don't need me anymore."

"PAPA!" I shouted. "Stop speaking this way. You're scaring me Papa!"

"Carmen! Basta! You are not me. I will always do what I want."

My father reached for his bottle of Grand Marnier and a small bottle bottle of pills. He took a few pills and a swig from the bottle.

"Grab my cigarettes off the table Carmen and leave me in peace."

With tears in my eyes, I did as I was told. I always did as I was told. Maybe that was the problem.

I went to my room and put on the radio. I knew what my father meant. He'd uttered strange things like this before while drinking, but there was such a sincere decisiveness in his voice. I fell back on my bed like the heroin junkies I saw shooting up in the coves of the streets in Hell's Kitchen, and closed my eyes.

I woke up to see my father passed out in his chair, with cigarette butts overflowing in the ashtray. I decided to wake up my father and see if he wanted to go to the movie theater with me and catch a show.

"No. Thank you Sonny Boy."

"There is a plate of food wrapped up for you on the table Papa."

"Thank you Sonny Boy," he slurred.

"Goodnight Papa."

I felt empty as I walked down 10th avenue to the theater where I worked. Each step was agony. My eyes were fixed to the sidewalk. I felt so lost in my life. There wasn't meaning anywhere. All I saw was a disgusting world that I lived in.

I greeted some of my co-workers, who didn't really know what all happened, but had probably heard from our boss. This explained why some fellow employees seemed abnormally friendly to me lately, but I just said, "Hello" and offered up no explanation, or emotion. I got a soda and some popcorn, then walked silently into the movie.

I felt nothing in the movie. I don't even remember what I saw. I just liked to sit in the dark theater and have the sounds and picture wash over me. At least it would take me out of my painful thoughts for some minutes here and there.

I walked home in the brisk air and still I felt emptier than when I was in the apartment. Each day and hour, it seemed as if my pain was becoming worse and even tangible. I dragged my legs up the stairs. Unlocked the door and turned the living room light on.

There was my father hunched over with an extension cord wrapped around his neck and the other end tied around a heating pipe. There was an open bottle of morphine pills on the table and the bottle was empty. He was cold to the touch. I broke down and fell to the feet of my father. I sobbed for what seemed like hours, pounding the floor and screaming. Our elderly neighbor, Rosetta, a short, stout woman from El Salvador was ringing our doorbell. I opened the door and fell into her arms.

I mumbled repeatedly, "He's dead, he's dead, he's dead."

Rosetta started crying softly and sang to me in Spanish.

We walked into our apartment and she gasped, but remained strong. We undid the extension cord from around my father's neck and leaned him back in the chair. I hugged my father as Rosetta called the police.

Within a couple of months I'd lost my parents. My only family, my best friends were now gone. I had nothing. My world had completely vanished. I felt nauseous. The burning in my stomach increased and I vomited all over the floor. I remained on all fours dry heaving as Rosetta hung up the phone and put her hand on my shoulder. She said we should go wait outside, but I rested my head on my father's legs and cried hysterically.

All I could feel was guilt. I could have prevented my mother being murdered. I could have prevented my father from committing suicide, but I failed them…again.

Was it now my turn to join them?

I had no one I could talk to. My only other friend was Yura. I called Yura from the hospital and he came to meet Rosetta and I. It was agreed that I would stay with Yura in Inwood indefinitely.

Chapter 7

Beautiful Struggle

My father once told me, "Sonny Boy, you can stay in the dirt waiting for crumbs, or you can stand and die like a man, because either way it turns and turns." Those words have never rang more true than now in this moment. I feel as if I'm nothing. I have no one. My only friend, and I'm terribly grateful for him as he's rescued me through music and countless other ways since I was a child, is a 67 year old Ukrainian cello teacher. For the last two weeks I've only been getting out of bed to go to the bathroom, make tea, and eat oatmeal. I listen to the radio most of the day.

Yura is very patient and he never had children of his own. Well, he told me he had one, but the child died during birth. He said those months when his wife was pregnant were the best months of his life. He was terribly in love with his wife of 5 years, Irina. They grew up together in Odessa and would walk along the water every morning before breakfast. She was a soprano and he said she had the most angelic voice he's ever heard, even to this day, but to be a singer was not in her destiny.

Yura told me she was going to Kiev for a concert and ended up falling in love with the Opera director. They'd known each other a long time, well all three of them had known each other a long time. Yura said, "I've never felt more betrayed in my life. Everything I knew and loved was no more. I was left with two choices Carmen, much like you right now. Well, we always have several choices, but there are always two main ones. Namely, stay, which usually means stay down like a dog that has been kicked in the ribs, or stand up and fight, go, run, whatever must be done. This is something similar to fight, or flight, an act that humans have been engaging in since the beginning of time."

Yura's wife had written him a letter and told him that she would not be returning home. He said it wasn't too long after, that he went on tour himself and decided to stay in America. He wasn't sure whatever happened to Irina, until a friend wrote him and said Irina and the director were hit head on by a drunk driver and died instantly. He started to cry as he told me the story and profusely apologized for telling me such a story, let alone at this time with all I must be going through.

I told Yura I was very sorry he had to experience that in life and I thanked him for opening up to me and in some strange way, it actually made me feel better. Maybe when we know about the pain others have went through, it actually helps us to cope with our own pain.

"Ok my friend, I must go downtown to teach. How about I bring us back some cannoli for tonight to go with our tea? Also, I have a piece of music I think you are ready to begin studying," said Yura.

"That sounds nice Yura. Thank you. I'll see you this evening then."

As soon as the door closed, I staggered back to my bed and engulfed myself in the blankets. I stared out the window and watched the clouds blow over Manhattan. I turned on the radio and listened to Hungarian Gypsy music. I decided since I hadn't left Yura's apartment in almost two weeks, I should go take a long walk around the Cloisters. This was one of my favorite spots in Manhattan.

The initial fresh air felt nice in my nostrils after being in Yura's apartment the last couple of weeks. However, every few steps felt nauseating as I was still processing the last few months. There was a constant state of feel great for 5 seconds, then remembering how much pain I was in for 10 seconds, which required the never ending task of reminding myself to keep going, even if only to pay homage to my parents.

I came to the cliff, past the Cloisters looking at the George Washington Bridge, and a sudden fleeting thought came and left my mind. I could feel an urge to walk out on that bridge and jump, or to jump from the cliff, to jump from anywhere, anything to end this ride and put an end to the physical, spiritual and mental anguish, but I knew I must carry on for something bigger than I could even begin to comprehend.

Upon leaving the park where I find peace and had taken an occasional walk with Yura over the years, I reminisce over the conversations we had as he told me about the many joys of touring, or the fantastic Opera houses and Ballets of Europe. "I loved the sound boots would make over cobblestone streets, as their non-punctual owners were walking briskly to the entrance, so as not to wait for intermission to take their seats."

I decided to walk down Dyckman to the chimichurri food truck that Yura would sometimes take me to after a lesson. These were the best Caribbean answers to the hamburger. The slightly sweet, oval bread over the thin grilled ground beef patties were delicious and I enjoyed them with a Mexican coca-cola everytime.

As I walked down Dyckman and heard the machine-gun fire Spanish of Domenicanos and the melodic flow of Boricuas, I started to compose a mini symphony in my head, when an image from a travel agency caught my attention. "Come to bella Italia," the poster stated. I could see some of the wonderful monuments of Italy in the poster and I started to wonder what life would be like for me, if I traveled there. I walked inside and inquired about a one-way to ticket to Palermo. The agent said they don't sell one-way tickets, unless they are for students, and she would need proof of student status, let alone they only fly to Rome. I told her I would be on student status and Rome would be fine. She said they were offering a deal for students at $149 each way. I asked her to place one ticket on hold and I would be back at the latest tomorrow afternoon to purchase the ticket. I walked outside of the travel agency and hurriedly walked to Yura's. I was so excited I forgot to get my chimichurri, and so I just ate oatmeal and drank Earl Grey tea with cream and a tablespoon of honey.

Yura opened his apartment door a few hours later and he was surprised to see me with a smile on my face, but then he started smiling.

"What's the great news my friend?" Yura asked.

"I saw a place that is selling a ticket to Rome for $149!" I exclaimed.

"Well, well. My Sicilian prodigal son is finally returning home," Yura said with a smile on his face.

"You're not mad?" I asked.

"Mad? Why would I be? I think it's great Carmen!" Yura said with excitement. "The only thing…what about your Juilliard audition? Didn't you want to go there?" Yura asked with a hint of concern, mixed with confusion in his tone.

"Of course I want to go to Juilliard Yura, but I don't know if I'm ready. Do you think they will give me an audition next year?" I asked.

Yura was silent a moment and then replied, "Let me go there tomorrow and speak to a friend of mine. I'll explain the situation and I'll see what I can do for you." Yura paused…" Now, I'm famished, let's go get a chimichurri."

I smiled. "Sounds great Yura! Let's go!"

As we walked down Dyckman, the smell of platanos permeated my nostrils. The reggaeton being blasted out of barber shops had an infectious rhythm that would often cheer me up. For me, some of the most authentic live moments would happen north of Central Park. I guess it had always been that way.

Yura explained that it would be a great experience to leave NY for the first time and make a life on my own. It would also be a blessing to see where my father grew up and just be in a warm climate.

"You can swim, eat great food, go for walks, listen to music, immerse yourself in a wonderful culture and history. There is a beautiful temple, still standing in great condition, Segesta and of course the mountain town of Erice! You will have a great time Carmen. Besides, who knows, if you stay there, I will come visit you and you can show me around."

"I don't know about living there, but we do still have some family there and I don't have any commitments here. You're my only friend Yura. The apartment will be sold soon as Arturo is handling that and any profit made will be set in an account for me. I'd like to give you some of the money, so you can take a vacation, or do whatever you want. Maybe you want to go visit Ukraine again."

"Nonsense Carmen! I appreciate the offer, but I don't want your money and I especially don't feel like visiting Ukraine right now, but still very sweet from you. That is your money for your future, for school, maybe a house of your own. I will be fine. Please don't worry about me Carmen. I want you to be happy!"

"Thank you Yura! You've always been so kind to me. I will never forget you!"

"Let's not get too sentimental, we still have chimis to order!"

As we walked home and stopped for a café con leche it occurred to me that this was the first time I felt alright and hopeful in life, at least in quite some time.

I told Yura I would go to the travel agency tomorrow and buy my ticket, as well as putting a rush on my passport. My goal would be to leave in a month, or so. Morning came and that is exactly what happened. Afterward I walked around Central Park. When I arrived at the spot where I had been severely beaten years prior, so many memories came flooding back. I went to a bench and started crying softly to myself. I knew I had to leave NY, at least for a few months. I would never heal and begin to become an adult, if I continued to remain complacent in Manhattan.

Chapter 8

Sicilia

The time to fly to Sicily was steadily approaching and my anticipation was mounting to levels previously unknown. I would stare at my ticket many times throughout the day. My passport arrived yesterday. I ran my fingers over the tough blue cover and felt the curved edges on my thumb. My thoughts ran adrift with all of the places I would travel to. I felt as if a key to the world was placed in my hands. I had scars on my soul. I had money in my pocket and the determination to heal and ultimately be a better man. I knew this would be a difficult journey, especially for a young man that's barely left his apartment in the last 20 years, but I also knew this journey was inevitable.

I had three days before I left NY. Yura returned home with a few surprises for me. Namely, sheet music of the Cello Sonata by Chopin, a Moleskin to write down my journey and a necklace with a small container to put the ash from my mother and father.

"I know their memories will forever be in you Carmen. This is a way to carry the physical as well. I hope this is ok for you Carmen."

"This is all very sweet Yura! Thank you. Thank you for everything. You've always treated me like family and I appreciate all that you've done for me. Thank you for the necklace too. I will carry them with me and I will also keep a diary of my travels. Thanks again Yura."

"C'mon Carmen. Let's make some dinner and go over this sheet music. Shall we?"

"Absolutely Yura!"

Yura prepared a local favorite when he was growing up called "fish head soup", which doesn't sound that appealing, but he is a great cook and I always enjoy eating with him albeit, fish head soup is an acquired taste.

After the meal, we sat down with our cellos and went through the Chopin piece. I remember Yura once telling me, "You know you have become a real musician when you feel every note and can play every note with passion, color and excitement, especially, when you do all of that with your eyes closed."

As we moved through the piece, it was as if my parents were in the room. I suddenly felt lightness in my body, peace in my soul, and for the first time, confidence. Well, a little confident, let's not get too crazy, but that was more than I'd ever had in my life before.

I can't explain clearly, but the notes became a part of me and I started to improvise upon them. They represented the soundtrack to my life. We became symbiotic. Eventually, I opened my eyes, as what I was playing was no longer the Chopin sheet music Yura had given me, and the astonished look on Yura's face told me I either did something horrible, or he loved it. Luckily, the latter was his feeling.

"What was that Carmen?" Yura asked.

"I don't know...I, uh...just played," I replied.

"Carmen. I've never heard you play with such confidence, such excitement, such, such...fury! That was improvisation. Yes? Your parents would be very proud of you for so many reasons right now. Please continue," said Yura.

"Thank you Yura. Thank you very much. Yes. I don't know what came over me, but I remember what you told me years ago and the stuff about closing my eyes. I became the music, or the music was the sound of my life…I just…I don't know, I've just never felt so connected to anything…I wish my parents were here to listen."

"They are Carmen. They are always here," Yura said softly with a smile and that Ukrainian twinkle in his eye.

We continued to play a while longer when Yura said it was time for a tea and baklava break. I couldn't argue with his wisdom, so we sat quietly in his kitchen listening to the radio, sipping our tea and nibbling on the sweet pastries. After a minute or two, Yura looked me directly in the eyes, "Carmen. I want you to know that I think you are doing the right thing by taking time to travel. I know your journey will not be an easy one, but I know you are making the right choice. If you are nervous, I want you to know not to be. As strange as this may seem to you now, I want you to know that you are blessed. You have been chosen for this difficult path that you've been forced to take and it will only make you stronger. It will take a long time to get through this, but I want you to know you will come out on top and I am always here for you. Ok?"

Yura's words made me choke up a bit and tears started to roll slowly down my cheeks.

"Thank you Yura. For everything you've ever done for me. I don't know where I would be without you in my life," I said softly.

We continued to sip our tea and finish our pastry.

"I think I will go to bed, Carmen. Sleep well my friend," Yura said with a smile.

"Thank you Yura. You too!" I replied.

As Yura walked off to his bedroom, I sat listening to the radio and let the music take me away from this life, much like the airplane would soon come to take me up and away from this life in NY.

In less than 48 hours, I would leave NY for the first time in my life. Yura and I spent the remaining time before I left NY walking through the Cloisters, Fort Tryon Park and Inwood Hill Park. If we weren't walking, we were going through the Chopin piece, improvising, listening to the radio while drinking tea and eating cannoli's. Yura would often joke he was an Eastern European man in his thinking, and an Italian in his stomach.

The day finally arrived when I got on the A train, to the E train and then finally the shuttle to JFK Airport. I made it through the airport and check in. We began to board the plane. I sat down in my seat by the window. As I looked out, I knew I'd never return the same again and that was fine. Within seconds, tears were streaming slowly, but steadily down my cheeks. I sat there quietly with my face looking out the window. My only wish at this moment, was that my parents were in the two seats beside me. I'd never ridden the train so far by myself, let alone through Queens, and here I am going to Europe by myself, taking my first flight, quite scared and nervous, but not questioning the inevitably of my destiny and pursuit of independence, with hope of finding peace and wisdom from my past.

Chapter 9

Rebirth

Flying for the first time was exhilarating. The feeling of ascension was like nothing I'd ever felt before. However, the tragic Polish, Sicilian catholic blood in me just felt terribly guilty, yet somehow, literally closer to the celestial home of my parents.

As the first leg of the journey had me landing in Paris, I was disappointed I didn't have the foresight to stay at least a couple of nights here. I made a mental note to come back, even if just to stay in a hostel, and busk upon the streets of Paris.

As I waited for my connecting flight to Palermo, my mind raced with memories, emotions and sensory overload. I was extremely excited and equally impressed with my own previously unseen courage to make this journey on my own, let alone with a one-way ticket and no guaranteed return date, or ticket for that matter.

I wondered, if I'd be recognized on the streets of Sicily by family, or friends from my father and if so, would that be a problem? I'd never met any of my father's family. He said it was best to stay away from all of them.

Over the years my mother told me stories of typical cliché, which I shall not repeat. Some stories that had carried over into the U.S., namely, La Mano Nera, but that "was a long time ago and your father has nothing to do with any of them. Although your grandfather insisted that your father work with his associates in the U.S., your father instead chose to carve out his own path, not involving himself in criminal activity. Of course, the opportunity to make a lot of money was present, but your father always stuck to his morals and principles. Your father always believed in the concept of Omertà, just not in organized crime," my mother once told me.

After being lost in my thoughts for minutes, the plane eventually took off and I was in the air for the first time of my life. I smiled looking out the window and felt so alive and free like never before. I wish my parents were here to see and experience this journey with me. I've basically talked to three people my entire life, so to not have any of them here would be extremely strange. I don't know what I would have done without Yura after the death of my mother and father. I probably would have went insane and killed myself. I felt so empty and helpless, so to actually feel alive and human again is extremely refreshing. I still break down almost every night when the evening sets in and the city sounds become sparse. I look out whatever windows are available, reflect and cry.

I took a deep breath through my nostrils as my feet hit the tarmac, and felt as if I was returning home after a terribly long journey. Shock was slowly setting in that I was no longer in NY. I didn't speak hardly any Italian and I didn't have any friends, or family to contact. Here I was 18 years old, not even old enough to legally drink in America and I was essentially now living in Sicilia, since I didn't have a return ticket, nor plans of returning. I accepted my self-created situation and proceeded to the tourist info desk. The woman at the desk was very helpful and spoke excellent English, which immediately put my mind at ease. I did as instructed and walked out of the airport to buy my bus shuttle ticket. After purchasing my ticket, I sat down and noticed a lot of people smoke cigarettes in Sicilia.

The bus arrived within 10 minutes and we were off to Palermo in another 5. I sat on the left side of the bus looking out over the various shades of the homes and into the rich blue hues of the Mediterranean. My eyes and senses were overwhelmed by the new colors, smells, sounds and climate that I was at this point unable to identify.

I stepped out of the bus at Piazza Politeama and felt an immediate thirst. I walked into a store and purchased the smallest cola I'd ever seen. The carbonated beverage was precisely 100ml, as big as my finger and just slightly above freezing. I sat down and enjoyed the burn from the bubbles slide down my throat. I sat in the piazza for about 15 minutes, before I started out walking toward my hostel. After another 15 minutes of pretty much unintentionally walking in a circle, I walked into a pharmacy, where the pharmacist spoke English and grabbed me by the wrist and walked the two minutes with me to the street where my hostel was.

After a "buona sera" and my meager attempt at small talk in Italian, I was given my key and escorted to my shared room. There happened to not be any other guests in my room that night, so I immediately took my shoes off and jumped into the top bunk and took a much needed nap. As I dozed off, I could hear the sounds of food frying, women shouting across the street to one another, an orchestra of car horns and mopeds whizzing by. Strangely enough, one of my last thoughts before falling asleep was the comparison of how it sounds like NY outside my window, and I dreamt of my old Hell's Kitchen childhood. I'd dreamt of my mother several times, but this night my father came to me for the first time in a dream. It felt so unbelievably real. My windows were open and the soft curtains were blowing against my exposed leg, when I felt my father sitting on the side of my bed, stroking my head, telling me softly, "Don't worry Sonny Boy, everything will be alright." I awoke suddenly, reaching out for my father, only to realize it was a dream, albeit, one of the most vivid dreams I'd ever had, but I immediately felt a sense of peace and understanding.

I decided to go walk around, as I was leaving in the morning on a short bus trip to visit Mondello, where my father was born, before coming back to Palermo to take the train to Trapani. As I walked around and worked my way through small cobblestone streets, narrow alleys, and aromas I'd yet to smell in my life, I was blown away by the wonderful backdrop of Palermo, the various shades of yellow of the buildings and the many street vendors offering up items I'd yet to ever see, let alone taste. I withdrew some Euros from my pocket and tasted one of the most amazing things I'd ever come across. Arancina, a wonderful fried rice ball, this one in particular stuffed with prosciutto and mozzarella, and was so incredibly delicious, I bought another one for later.

I sat down in a small piazza with a couple of cafes in its square and I ordered a Peroni. I sipped on my beer and thought it was funny that in the U.S. this would definitely not happen, as I would probably either not be allowed in a bar, even in

Manhattan, let alone nonchalantly order a beer. So there I was enjoying myself in solitude. My symphony was the street's orchestral sounds, and as always, the life is and was outside. I'd never seen such an array and concentrated quality of women walking with such air and class, I couldn't stop watching their gait.

I decided to walk around and find a church to pray. I haven't prayed since my mother passed away. She would always pray with me and read Psalms to me. We weren't Catholic, but very faithful and she always encouraged me to read the Bible and follow my heart, so I let my feet lead my body. After a few twists and turns, I wandered into a small, but beautiful church. The floor was covered in an ancient, exquisite mosaic. I always loved mosaic, as my father had shown me pictures of the famous mosaics of Ravenna. He would laugh at me when I told him I would move there and make the most beautiful mosaic on Earth.

I sat down quietly and closed my eyes. I felt a sense of relief that I didn't know I was carrying. I stayed in the pew for about 10 minutes, before walking out into the evening warmth. I picked up a small, fresh tuna sandwich on the way home and awoke in my clothes, covered in crumbs and an oily wrapper on my face.

I packed up my items in the morning, checked out and walked but a hundred feet before finding a spot to eat breakfast. I ordered a pastry and a latte macchiato.

After finishing my light breakfast I walked back to Piazza Politeama and waited for my bus to Mondello. As we exited the city, bright green covered trees appeared on both sides of the road where rays of sunshine would break through and end on the pavement. Within no time, we arrived in Mondello and I got out and threw my backpack over my left shoulder. Within one minute, I was on the boardwalk and ordered a gelato. I sat down in the usually sleepy suburb of Palermo, yet in summertime, the area was full with locals and a large amount of tourists. I took in the summer resort towns atmosphere and walked around for a few hours where I stumbled upon a secret beach, which only cost 50 cents admission. I took off my shoes, socks and t-shirt. I rolled up my khaki pants and jumped in the turquoise water. I'd felt reborn and energized as I sat on a rock, letting the sun dry my thin pants.

I walked around Mondello some more and imagined my father swimming at the beach in town, or running up and down the streets playing with his siblings. I could almost hear their laughter. It was at this moment my bus back to Palermo arrived. I felt at peace as we made our way back to Palermo. I felt as if my father was at peace too. How I longed to see my parents though. How I wished to speak with them. How I would do anything to have them here with me at this moment, at every moment, but then reality set in and I knew I was setting myself up for wishes that would not manifest.

I made it back to my room and felt an immense emptiness, that I was worried would never truly disappear. I also knew I had to keep moving, otherwise how could I honor my parents. I wasn't sure what I was looking for, but I knew I was in the right place.

Morning had arrived, and I'd said but a few sentences in the last few days, which was lonely, but great for self-reflection. I made my way to Palermo Stazione Centrale and purchased my ticket. I felt terribly sad in the sunshine. I felt tremendously alone. I decided to buy a beer, a bottle of water and a sandwich. I slammed my beer, ate my sandwich and walked back to the train station. I'd never been on a train other than the NY subway system, so I was excited for this mini adventure.

Within 30 minutes of travel, tears started pouring down my cheeks. I sat silently, as I was overwhelmed by the beauty of the island from where my father came from. A few hours later and we arrived in Trapani. I walked at a snail's pace before a gorgeous woman began speaking to me. I thought she liked me, but I suddenly realized she was a Rumanian prostitute and just wanted 50 euros for sex. Still being a virgin, I politely declined her offer, as this wasn't how I imagined losing my virginity. She was extremely pretty though. It was still nice to have a conversation with another human.

I found my small hotel room, where I immediately set my bag down and jumped in a hot shower. I felt much better afterward and decided to get some dinner. My meal was not a disappointment. The grilled octopus over couscous accompanied by a nice glass of red wine had my belly full and my eyes sleepy. I returned to my room and fell fast asleep. I woke up in a daze and knew I would go to the town my father told me was "the most beautiful place on Earth."

After breakfast of salsiccia, bread, mozzarella, juice and four espressos, I was ready to make my journey. It took about an hour and several questions in my poor Italian to find the bus stop to San Vito Lo Capo. As I was waiting patiently with my legs exposed in the sunshine and my torso in the shade, leaning back against the cream-colored stucco wall, a lime fell and hit my head. Awakened from my day-dream I bent down to pick the lime off of the ground and as I did that, a second lime fell and hit me. I picked up the second yet to be ripe lime, rolled it through my fingers, and felt how firm it was. At that moment, the bus arrived and I hurriedly stuffed the limes in my pocket. I boarded the bus, paid my fare and took a seat by the window.

As the bus wove through the streets of Trapani, I looked out along the beautiful view, which was composed of a blend of various shades of turquoise, lined with beaches full of soft caramel colored sand. I suddenly had a vision of these limes, my childhood, my parents, and the last 18 years speeding through my mind in a matter of seconds. I started to cry quietly on the bus. I took out a black marker I had and drew a small rendition of my mother's face on the first lime that fell. I rather liked my drawing, in exception of when we hit a bump and I smeared her left eyeball a bit, but the face still came out well. Next, I started drawing my father on the second lime. After I was finished I admired my work briefly and gently placed the two limes in my bag, leaned my head back, and stared peacefully out of the large window onto the beautiful hills of Sicily.

I had no solid plan, or intention of what I was to do in Sicily, but I knew I had to be there. I often felt a déjà-vu feeling, which is strange for someone that spent the majority of their waking hours in an apartment playing cello to the point of obsession. The landscape of western Sicily was like nothing I'd ever seen before. The large, roaring hills, the trees scattered throughout, the beautifully quaint homes and their yards spotted with vines, shade and more beautiful trees and flowers. I looked at the lime with the face of my mother and whispered, "I wish you could see this too mama." I held the lime tight and more tears began to flow.

Our bus proceeded to weave through hills and winding streets. Occasionally, we would stop in small towns for passengers to board the bus. The people appeared to be either workers heading to San Vito Lo Capo, or young teenagers already displaying the passion of a Sicilian couple. The intense look into the eyes of your lover. The kisses that can make you forget all space and time. The joking and banter that goes from loving to agitation, back to love within seconds, was infectious for the autonomous citizens of the largest island in the Mediterranean. How I longed to have had a girlfriend, hell to have even kissed a woman at this point would've been amazing, but I shifted my thoughts to the scenery passing by my window. I reached into my bag and pulled out a soft yellow fruit, to which I've unfortunately forgot the name, but I'll always remember the taste. I washed that down with a long swig of sparkling water.

The last image of my father would frequently enter my mind, or the image of my mother and how I imagined her fighting off her attacker. I wondered if these thoughts and images would ever leave my conscious, or was I destined to be confined to the constant reminder of how they suffered in life, their death, and into their afterlife. I only hoped that my parents were happy now.

The bus drifted on around a slow curve and I could tell we were approaching San Vito Lo Capo, as we'd been on the road nearly an hour, and the town my father described as the most beautiful thing, other than my mother, was within a few minutes reach. The bus stopped by a large group of street vendors and the passengers poured out of the bus as if they were late for an important meeting. Myself, being in a perpetual state of aloofness and no real sense of time, or urgency, let everyone exit before me. I took a deep breath and set my feet onto the soil where my father told me his family would sometimes take a weekend trip in the summertime. I felt closer to my papa at this time, more than ever. I wish he were here now and I could remember a smile on his face, instead of the disoriented look that stayed on his face the last couple of weeks of his life.

I walked past the vendors and proceeded toward the beach. When I was within sight of the most beautiful water I'd seen, in pictures, or in person, I dropped to my knees and began to cry like never before. I cried for my parents. I cried for all of the hate in the world. I cried for anyone that was poor and left their family, their country, their home in search of a better financial life, which doesn't always equate to a better quality of life. I cried for anyone that had truly suffered. I had my head in my hands for a few minutes. I didn't care if anyone saw me crying. I gathered my composure after truly realizing how odd I must have appeared and walked toward the water. I could hear the voices of caramel colored men attempting to sell their wares, drinks and snacks, all the while cigarettes hanging from their lips. I'd only been to a beach a few times in my life and it was nothing like what I experienced on that day. I was never speechless from the beauty of the moment when I went to Brighton Beach and I was an easily amused recluse.

I threw my t-shirt onto my backpack and slowly walked into the water. I walked for about 100 feet, and pretended that my soul would be cleansed by jumping into the water. I dove in and as I ascended I thought that I'd not felt this great in a long time. For the first time in months I felt alive. The pain I'd been carrying with me on a constant basis since the murder of my mother was now lessening. I swam for her. I swam for my father. I swam for peace of my own mind, and when I burst through the water and came up to the surface, the sun penetrating through that lovely shade of blue, for just a moment in time, everything was alright in life.

I walked to a supermarket and bought an ice cold Peroni, scampi, bread and olives. After awhile, I decided to go walk around outside of town and find a place where I could put my mat down and take a nap. I walked past small hostels, RV's and what appeared to be a small campground. The town seemed very relaxed and peaceful and I immediately felt at ease. I continued to walk outside of town and into the hills. The heat was rising, as well as my pulse, but I felt great. I stopped and took a long drink of water and watched three birds fly over the sea completely at peace. I imagined those birds to be my parents and me. I looked down and tears started streaming down my face. I whimpered quietly, not that the sound mattered as I hadn't seen another person for at least a mile, but I still felt as if I was a wounded animal hiding from predators.

I started to walk back to town when it occurred to me that I could just sleep under a tree and save money on a hostel, or a campground. I figured I was on an island, so I couldn't imagine there were many snakes, or scorpions on the ground, so at least I would be somewhat safe. I would bathe in the sea, and since I could just buy food from the market, cooking wasn't really an issue, so I would try to sleep under the stars as long as possible.

One great thing I missed, for which I had no viable solution, was my lack of access to playing and creating music. The cello isn't exactly the most portable instrument. Yet I had some sheet music to study, a journal to write in and the music of so many wonderful pieces committed to memory. I was hoping I would find a local cellist that would let me play their instrument occasionally, but for now I walked.

For several days I carried on my tradition of sleeping on the ground, and in the morning, walking into town to buy breakfast and snacks to keep me nourished throughout the day, as well as a giant bottle of water. I was able to keep my daily costs to a little over $10 U.S., which certainly wasn't possible in Manhattan, so I was already profiting financially, let alone mentally and spiritually by being in Sicily.

It occurred to me that I hadn't spoken aloud in 3 days. I was starting to feel a little lonely, but I didn't have a care in the world, other than looking out over the sea from the shade of my favorite tree that I'd found. I started to draw a picture of the sea and surrounding landscape, when I thought I could take out my two limes with the faces of my parents drawn upon them and have a "conversation".

Talking to two limes with primitive drawings of my parents faces didn't seem all that strange to me. I mean, no one was around anyway, so what did it matter if I spoke to a couple of limes that I pretended to be my parents. I wasn't hurting anyone, and after a few minutes it did make me feel better, and the loneliness started to fade.

I told my parents of my journey and how happy I was in Sicily. I told them that I hoped they were proud of me for being able to navigate a country that I'd never been to. I thought this was a pretty significant achievement for a nerdy, awkward, young man, that not too long ago couldn't even ride a bike without training wheels.

I thought I would give my parents a tour of the lovely area I now called home. I walked by the wild trees and flowers that I couldn't identify. I knew my mother would love it here. I walked by the edge of a small cliff, and as fast as that thought entered my mind, I tripped over a small stone. My natural reaction was to hold the limes and protect them the way I was never able to protect my parents on Earth. I fell hard and could taste metal in my mouth. A taste I was familiar with due to the frequent beatings I got from my angry peers in NY.

I dropped the lime that was my mother. I watched it fall into the beautiful multi-shades of blue. I immediately broke down and started sobbing. I was weeping uncontrollably for minutes. The symbolism of me losing that lime stood for every fatal mistake I made the night my mother was murdered. I knew I'd failed her. I failed my father and I was to live with these thoughts the rest of my life.

I sat there for many more minutes staring at my bloody knee and hand. I felt empty. I felt hopeless. I felt alone. Yura was my only friend that I spoke to now and he was thousands of miles away and I wasn't near a phone. I cried myself to sleep and awoke with a terrible sunburn. I stood up and dragged my body to town. I wished I was normal. I longed to be like the people in my neighborhood that appeared to be on top of the world, fearless. There was nothing courageous, or all that remarkable about me. My cello was all I had in life and since I didn't have that, I felt incomplete and useless.

I bought a bottle of water, two Peroni's, bread and cheese. I walked back to my makeshift camp as the sun was setting. I felt the stares of local townspeople watching me with a type of curiosity, more likely probably wondering how a young man could be in such a beautiful place, with a look of misery on his face. I wondered that too, but it wasn't easy for me to heal. I walked on and hummed Chopin to myself.

I made it back to my area, which was already displaying the worn out ground as if a pack of animals had been living there. I figured I should probably move tomorrow when I awoke, just to not stay anywhere too long and be that noticeable.

I felt better when the sun came up. I stared in the dark abyss most of the night, as I did in NY on most nights, only here there wasn't any light pollution, so to see into nothing, was as if I was peering into my own soul and it felt painfully at home with the depressive thoughts in my soul. Nevertheless, I packed up my items and put all of my trash into a white plastic bag and began to wander. I found a nice hill overlooking San Vito Lo Capo and I decided to set up my makeshift home under a nice tree which bore a fruit I was unfamiliar with.

It was around the 10 day mark of not speaking to anyone as I sat alone in my thoughts, humming music to myself and drawing sketches in my notebook, when I decided to talk to my father. I pulled out the lime with the worn out marker which was now beginning to smear the face of my father. I spoke openly to my "father" like never before. I explained to him that I wished I was never home-schooled. I told him how hard it was to be his son. I told him that I felt like I was never good enough for him. I wasn't strong enough, fast enough, smart enough, stable enough. I knew he loved me, but he had such a funny way of showing it. I told him I thought he was too hard on my mom and myself and I never understood why. It seemed the only thing he never criticized was my musicianship. I told him that I wished he would've said he loved me. I also asked why he never showed me how to ride a bike, or at least teach me when I was a child. I never understood why we lived in NY, but led such a sheltered life, but most importantly I thanked him for caring. I certainly could never criticize his display of care. My father did everything for my mother and I. He always made sure we were taken care of. I can't imagine the pain and emptiness he must've felt when my mother passed. I guess I can almost understand him committing suicide. I just wanted to see them again, and to know it's not a possibility, left me emptier than ever. I continued to speak to my father and tell him about my time in

Sicily. I held the lime to the sun in the sky as I spoke in merrier tone than just a few minutes ago.

It was at that time I heard the voices of young, drunk, British tourists making fun of me. I'm not sure how long they'd been there, but they were within 10 feet of me.

"What the fuck are you doing mate?" said the tallest and largest of their group.

"Have you gone mental? What a fucking wanker!" yelled the chubby one.

"Why are you here? Are you like homeless, or something?" snarled the ugly, dark-haired monster.

"Are you going to fucking answer us, or what?" the large beast of a Brit asked.

I just stared at them. I was familiar with this scenario and I knew what was inevitable if I said something.

"Well. Speak up you fucking wanker! Why the fuck are you talking to a lime? Are you fucking mad?" snarled their drunk, ignorant leader.

Tears were forming in my eyes. I've never bothered anyone. I don't seek stress. I have enough pain and misery to last me two lifetimes. My eyes drifted to the ground.

I tasted metal, and felt a thud in my chest, as my eyes went from staring at the ground silently to now the bright blue sky. My back landed on a rock and I could feel it cut into my back. My arms hit the ground, and I felt the lime fall from my hand. I knew it landed in the Mediterranean. Much like my mother that I couldn't protect, I'd now lost my father. In a matter of seconds I knew I had two choices; continue to be complacent and subservient or stand up for myself. For the first time in my life, I chose the latter.

With rage burning through my veins, and the fury of ancient Cartucci bloodlines, I jumped to my feet and a voice in my head said, "Temple...kill shot." I listened to that voice, and with everything I had, I threw the first punch of my life and landed it on their fearless leader. He dropped like that lime to the sea seconds ago. His goons proceeded to throw swings and kicks. The adrenaline of fighting was like nothing I'd ever felt. I felt so alive and proud of myself for finally standing up to violence and ignorance. I fought the best I could, but I was outnumbered and not an experienced fighter. By the time their leader stood and used a stone for a fist filler to deliver the blow that caused me to black out, I was already delirious with joy, pain and laughter. The look on their faces as I laughed was of a frightened child, as if they knew they were battling a mad man. They hit and kicked me harder as if they were outnumbered. Blood was already pouring from my head, and iron was the taste in my mouth, as I went down, though I knew I'd won the fight. I fought back. I was the victor today. For the first time in my life I truly felt unstoppable, and then the lights turned off.

I must've been lying there nearly a day when I slowly awoke to warm water on my forehead and lips. I heard the soothing, soft humming of what sounded like a children's song. I was able to open my left eyelid just slightly. Everything was burning with pain and soreness.

"Grazie", I was able to mutter. I knew I was missing some teeth as my tongue pushed into emptiness.

"Prego uomo dolce." Said the woman with the most beautiful voice I'd ever heard.

I could barely lift my head. I couldn't move my right arm. I could wiggle both of my legs, and my left hand felt like it went through a blender, but I knew it was worth it, as I'd landed some shots on the ignorant thugs.

"What's your name?" I asked.

The beautiful woman smiled and tried to imitate what I said, "Wuzzurnam".

She looked confused.

"Nome?" I asked.

"Ah. Capito," she said. "Me name are Angelica," she said softly.

An angel she was indeed. I smiled.

"Grazie mille Angelica." I said.

She smiled from ear to ear and continued to clean my head. Angelica fed me these small pieces from a yellow fruit that looked like a little tomato. It was sweet and the taste made me forget the pain for just a minute. I reflected at losing my parents in real life, and that I even lost the inanimate versions of them as well. I felt terribly sad, but happy that I made a new friend. Well, sort of. She probably just pitied me, but nevertheless, it was nice to have company, especially after just receiving the most severe beating of my life.

"Who you?" Angelica asked.

"My name is Carmino Cartucci. I'm from New York."

"Ah Carmino Americano?"

"Mi padre Siciliano," I uttered in pain, yet trying to sound sweet and flirt.

"Benvenuto a casa," she said in the sweetest tone.

I smiled. She stood and spoke rapidly in an accent I couldn't fully understand, but something about family and her mother, then she waved goodbye.

I started to cry from the pain, as my body crumpled when I attempted to go after her. I cried for losing another person in my life, tears rushing down my face just like the people I loved rushed out of my life. I cried for life. I cried for the weak. I cried for those suffering. I just fucking cried. I felt lighter. I felt better. I fell asleep.

I awoke startled to a soft kiss on my head and a light touch on my right shoulder.

"Everything will be ok sonny boy," said my father. Unfortunately, it was a dream so real I awoke confused. It still hurt to move, but I heard footsteps and tightened up. I was relieved when my friend Angelica returned. She poured water down my throat and then gave me some mocha from a small metal container. After a few minutes she held out her hand. I smiled and together with her help I stood. We locked eyes and I knew she was the one. I took one look over my shoulder at the place where I'd spent so many pivotal days and I knew I was a man. I knew I was reborn. I knew I'd heal from loss. I knew I must continue to put one foot in front of the other. I knew my parents needed me to carry on. I knew I had a lot to give to the world. Today was the first day of my life.

Angelica looked at me and smiled. In a soft tone, "Carmino Americano," she said.

"My angel Angelica," I said.

As the sun was setting, we held hands and slowly walked down the path to San Vito Lo Capo, the most beautiful place on Earth.

Made in the USA
Columbia, SC
15 March 2019